Henry Bate

The Rival Candidates

A Comic Opera in Two Acts - As it is Now Performing at the Theatre Royal

in Drury-Lane

Henry Bate

The Rival Candidates
A Comic Opera in Two Acts - As it is Now Performing at the Theatre Royal in Drury-Lane

ISBN/EAN: 9783337069599

Printed in Europe, USA, Canada, Australia, Japan

Cover: Foto ©Andreas Hilbeck / pixelio.de

More available books at **www.hansebooks.com**

THE

RIVAL CANDIDATES:

A COMIC OPERA

In Two ACTS;

AS IT IS NOW PERFORMING AT THE

THEATRE ROYAL

IN

DRURY-LANE.

———————————

By the Rev. HENRY BATE.

———————————

LONDON:

Printed : Sold by T. BECKET, corner of the
Adelphi - buildings, in the Strand ; and by
W. GRIFFIN, No. 6, Catharine-ftreet,

DEDICATION.

To Mrs. GARRICK.

MADAM!

PERHAPS you were not aware, when you were kind enough to fhew an early countenance to the following *petite* OPERA, that fo indulgent an overture, entitled it in fome meafure to your future patronage; indeed, notwithftanding this circumftance, you might probably have efcaped the prefent mortifying fituation, had not the author conceived, that his piece owes no inconfiderable fhare of its dramatic effect to your tafte and judgment:—hence arofe an appeal to his feelings, too powerful to be treated with filent indifference.—

I mean not, however, to alarm your delicacy, by a recital of thofe accomplifhments, which have long rendered you an ornament of the moft fafhionable circles;——nor by recounting thofe private virtues, which ftamp you one of the firft patterns of domeftic felicity; facts however agreeable or inftructive they might prove to fociety, I decline enumerating, in compliment to female diffidence.

Having

DEDICATION.

Having therefore made the acknowledgement I conceive due upon this occasion, it is high time for me frankly to confess, that vanity had some influence over me, when I presumed to think of Mrs. GARRICK for the patroness of this my FIRST ESSAY.

I remain Madam,

with great respects

Your most obedient,

and devoted Servant,

Hendon, Middlesex,
Feb. 9, 1775.   HEN. BATE.

ADVERTISEMENT.

THE RIVAL CANDIDATES is an attempt of the dramatic kind, undertaken by the writer from no motive of literary vanity, but in order to introduce to the world, a young mufical compofer, whofe tafte he conceived might do honour to his profeffion.

The reformer of the Englifh drama no fooner was informed of him, than he kindly confented to an early trial of his abilities, and difcovered a ge-nerous anxiety for his fuccefs.

The author arrogates to himfelf but a moderate fhare of that univerfal applaufe with which his piece has been received, particularly when he re-collects how much of it is derived from the kind attention of Mr. GARRICK, in the double capacity, of friend, and manager;—and what immenfe claims thofe refpectable perfons have, who fill his little canvafs with fuch credit to themfelves, and their profeffion. To fingle out any one of thefe celebrated performers, when all fo kindly combined to produce, what is deemed a ftriking repre-fentation in the comic ftyle, would be a tafk un-pleafing as ungenerous. And therefore, as they have been equally zealous in their endeavours, as happy in the execution of their feveral characters, he wifhes them, jointly to accept, the returns of a grateful heart.

DRA-

DRAMATIS PERSONÆ.

Byron,	Mr. Vernon.
Sir Harry Muff,	Mr. Dodd.
General Worry,	Mr. Parſons.
Spy,	Mr. Weſton.
First Gardener,	Mr. Banniſter.
Under Gardeners,	{ Mr. Kear, { Mr. Fawcett.
Narcissa,	Mrs. Baddely.
Jenny,	Mrs. Wrighten.

SCENE, A Country Villa, &c.

THE

RIVAL CANDIDATES.

ACT. I   SCENE I.

A Hall in General WORRY's *houfe, adorned with mili-
tary trophies; through the folding doors of which, is feen
a part of the garden.*

NARCISSA and JENNY.

Jenny. ———INDEED ma'm I don't like to go
near him :—befides, what the deuce
fhould he want with me?

Nar. Oh fome frefh complaints, I'll warrant you :—
but I defire you'd go.

Jenny. Lud ma'm! he's fuch an old fufpicious mor-
tal, that I can do no good with him :—and its a fhame
to throw away good reafoning, and fine fentiment,
upon fo unfeeling a ———

Nar. Prithee, don't be trifling now, girl, but go
to him, and let us know the worft.

Jenny. Well, to oblige you, ma'm, I'll venture any
thing.

[*Exit* Jenny.

B   Nar-

- Narciſſa *alone.*

Why was I doom'd to envy the free-born villager?—
or what do I derive from fortune or education, but
reflections, which render my confinement inſupport-
able.—The family quarrel which ſeparates me from
the man I love, and my father's unreaſonable ſuſpicions lie heavy on my ſpirits :—deny'd even to breathe
that pure air, which nature deſigned as a common bleſ-
ſing to all her creatures!—Surely the time will come
when I ſhall regain my liberty, and my *Byron* have an
opportunity of refuming the tender ſubject of his paſ-
ſion, ſo cruelly cut off in its infancy.

A I R I. *Mrs. Baddely.*

Soft FANCY thou truant to me,
    My ſummons oh quickly obey!
Neglected by BYRON and thee,
    How heavily paſſes the day!

Thy charms I've miſtaken for Love's,
    So artfully doſt thou beguile,
Thy magic enlivens the groves,
    When he has forgotten to ſmile!

Enter JENNY *haſtily.*

Jenny. Oh dear, ma'm!—charming news, ma'm!

Nar. Thou art a mad girl :—but what is the cauſe
of this tranſport?

Jenny. Lud m'am! as I hope to live and breath,
your papa is going down to the borough to vote for his
friend, Mr. *Indigo*, the Nabob, and his nephew, Sir
Harry Muff, the ſweet ſpark that lines his clothes with
fur in the dog-days—and your lover that is to be—

Nar.

Nar. My love that is to be!—but prithee go on—

Jen. And so, ma'm, he has given us leave to divert ourselves in the plantations, till he returns:—he sent *Spy* in search of you, to tell you of it before he saw me.

Nar. Indeed!

Jen. Yes, indeed, and indeed, Ma'm!—I wish I could let *somebody* know of it, that—he might pay us a visit.

Nar. That's impossible, *Jenny*:—but soft!—here comes my father's cabinet counsellor.

Enter SPY.

Nar. ——Well, Sir, what's your business?

Spy. Business, madam!—no great matter of business truly; only his worship ordered me to tell you, that he was going to the election at *Tipplewell*; and so if you thought fit, you and Mrs. *Jenny* might re-create yourselves in the pleasure grounds (as it's a fine day) till he returns.

Jen. There's kindness for you, madam!

Spy. But he charg'd me to tell you, he'd have no lolling out of the summer-house window that looks to the high-road;—nor no singing, for fear you should scare the wild-ducks that are hatching in the island;—nor no——

Jen. ——Opening our eyes, I suppose, for fear we should see any thing in the shape of a man!—now your bolt's shot!—Your master's very kind truly, after depriving us of every enjoyment for three months past, he now sets a dish before us, and generously tells us we must not taste of it.

Spy.

Spy. Why you know, Mrs. *Jenny,* I would refuſe you nothing ; not even if you were to take a liking to me myſelf.

Jen. That would be a fine diſh indeed!

Nar. Come, come, no more of this ; you may tell your maſter, I think myſelf obliged to him, even for this limited indulgence :—what does the fellow ſtand ſo like a ſtatue for ?

Spy. I only waits to let you in, that's all.

Nar. You may ſave yourſelf that trouble, by giving the keys to my maid.

Jen. Come give them to me, Sir.—

Spy.—But axing your pardon, Miſs *Narciſſa,* that's not the caſe neither ; I was ordered to lock the garden doors after you, and carry the keys back to your papa.

Nar. Lock us in, for what ?

Jen. Ay, for what, Sir ?

Spy. For—for—oh !——only for fear the turkies ſhould get in, and eat up all the ſtrawberries, that's all.

Nar. I underſtand my father's cruel ſuſpicions ; but thou haſt more delicacy than thy maſter ; go open the gates.

[Exit Spy.

Jen. Now, ma'm !—if Mr. *Byron* be the gentleman I take him for, he'll find it out—ſome how or other that the old gentleman has left his watch, and be here in the twinkling of an eye.——

Nar. Ah Jenny ! 'tis three long weeks—

Jen. So it is Ma'm, ſince he blew you the laſt kiſs from the orchard-wall, by moonlight :—I'm ſure it

almoſt

almoſt melted my heart, it was ſent up with ſuch a deep
ſigh :—poor young gentleman !—I wiſh I was not of
ſo tender a conſtitution myſelf in theſe caſes.

Nar. Heigh day !—why I ſhall look upon thee as my
rival preſently :—Well, I muſt confeſs girl, that Byron
finds in thee a powerful advocate, and I, a faithful con-
fidante : I hope we ſhall be enabled to reward thy fidelity.

Jen. I ſhould be ſufficiently repaid, Ma'm, in ſeeing
you happy :—dear me ! if he would but come now and
offer himſelf a candidate here, we might have a ſnug
little election of our own :—he ſhould have my vote,
and if I know any thing of eyes, I don't think, but
you'd immedlately return him.

Nar. Faith, I cannot ſwear that I wou'd not, Jenny.

Jen. Lord, Ma'm !—I can eaſily clamber over the
pales if they do lock us in :—let me go then, and ſee
if I can find him any where.

Nar. Heavens, girl, not for the world !—after ſuch
an imprudent advance on my part, I need not wonder
if a cool indifference ſhould ſucceed on his : for I have
been told, Jenny, that men always ſet a value upon a
conqueſt, in proportion to the eaſe, or difficulty with
which it is obtain'd :—and yet I long to ſee him !—but
come, I am impatient to enjoy once more the beauties
of nature : I am going into the drawing-room for my
book ; you'll find me at one of my favourite ſeats,
where I really long to reſt myſelf.   [*Exit Nar.*

JENNY, *alone.*

Poor young lady !—I wonder ſhe holds it out ſo long :
no ſleep o'nights, and her little heart hurry ſcurry,
hurry ſcurry, all day :—the deuce take the men ſay I,
for a pack of unfeeling numſkulls ; they are all alike—
won-

wonderfully loving, when locks and bars are between; but if you give 'em a favourable opportunity, not one in ten of them has the brains to make ufe of it.

A I R II. *Mrs. Wrighten.*

Fie! fie! filly man,
Your foft nonfenfe forego,
No heart you'll trepan
With your fighing—heigho!
For that's not the way a fond damfel to woo;
A truce to your whining,
Your fobbing, and pining;
But prefs her!
Carefs her!
The bufinefs is done, and fhe'll foon buckle too.

[*Exit Jenny.*

SCENE

SCENE II.

Enter GENERAL WORRY, *discovering* JENNY *as she goes off.*

Gen. There's a baggage for you now!—Zounds! if I had ftole a march upon her a minute fooner, I fhould have catch'd 'em out!—Damme, if the life I now lead is not more perilous, than when I was upon the coaft of France, and expeéted a mine to be fprung upon me every ftep I advanced.—A fine bouncing girl, fcribbling dying fongs, and love letters, from morning till night, and fnivelling day after day for *Liberty*, in order to run away with fome fcape-grace, who'll cut my throat to get in for my fortune;—and an abigail, crafty enough to debauch the morals of a Lapland virgin!—It's too much for an invalid of fixty-five!—But, upon fecond thought, there can come no great harm on letting them out for a little while:—befides it will give Narciffa a bloom againft I bring Sir Harry home with me:——

[*Enter* SPY, *whiftling, and leading a large maftiff.*
Spy. Here, Dragon! Dragon!
Gen. Well Spy!—what have you let 'em out?
Spy. Yes, your honor's worfhip, I let 'em loofe:—it would have done your heart good to fee 'em: they jump'd and frifk'd about, for all the world, like rabbits in a warren.
Gen. But did you double-lock all the gates?
Spy. Yes, your honor: and I've unmuzzled Dragon, and am going to let him loofe in the back yard.

Gen.

Gen. Well, that's right; but fuppofe they fhould clamber over the pales and elope? I've heard of fuch things in my time!

Spy. So have I; but they muft fcramble deucedly if they do;—indeed, for the matter of that, Mrs. Jenny has a fine ftride with her.

Gen. Are you fure now, Spy, that you've feen no fufpicious kind of body lurking about the grounds this week paft?

Spy. Not a foul, indeed, your honor; nor can I track any thing but the foot of farmer Brown's Tom cat, that comes caterwauling after Mifs Narciffa's Tabby; and, if I catch him, I fancy I fhall ftop his rambles.

Gen. Well then, all's well!—but I'm wafteing time here—I'll fet out—nothing fhould have tempted me from home, but the fear of affronting my old friend *Indigo*: —Sir *Harry* will have a fine eftate, in a ring-fence, clofe to mine,—he's worth a little powder.—Come *Spy*, you and Dragon to your pofts:—you muft have an hawk's eye upon 'em;—and be fure you don't tipple upon guard:—behave like a foldier to day, and I'll give you leave to get drunk to morrow by day break.

Spy. Thank your honor, I'll take you at your word: [*going returns*] your worfhip [*pointing to Dragon*] we are a pair of ftaunch friends, or deadly enemies.

[*Exit with Dragon.*]

Gen. —Now I recollect, there is certainly a confpiracy againft me, for I traced a man's foot upon the tulip-bed, a full inch longer than *Spy's* or any of the gardeners.—If I find her out, I don't know what I fhall do in my paffion!—perhaps take a fecond rib, and get a fon and heir to difinherit her!

AIR

AIR III. *Mr. Parfons.*

What new curfes fpring up,
'To replenifh man's cup,
'Tho' heaven in pity has borrowed his wife !
His daughter will grieve him,
With plots to deceive him :
But mine !—oh, I'll match her
The firft time I catch her,
Attempt, a young jade, to embitter my life !

[*Exit.*

C   SCENE

SCENE III.

NARCISSA *difcovered on a garden feat reading :*—JENNY *entering haftily to her with a bird.*

Jen. Law, ma'm!—I have caught the fweeteft little linnet in the green-houfe, that ever you faw in all your born days :—how it's little heart goes pit-a-pat !—only look at it, ma'm :—

Nar. Depriv'd of liberty myfelf, I cannot behold the pretty captive without emotion :— prithee, let it go :———

Jen. But perhaps we may never catch it again, ma'm :—and I want to hang it up as a companion to my little bull-finch.

Nar. The generous find more true delight in reftoring their prifoners to freedom, than in all the advantages they derive from their captivity :—Pretty fportive creatures !—tho' we envy them their liberty, never let it be faid, that we invade the fmalleft of their little privileges.

[*While the fymphony is playing, Jenny releafes the bird.*]

A I R IV. RONDO. *Mrs. Baddely.*

Love unfetter'd is a blefling
    Nature's commoners enjoy ;
Source of raptures paft expreffing,
    Which no tyrant laws deftroy.

Come

Come ye fongfters ! wing around me,
Tell me all ye know of love :
Watchful of your young you've found me ; —
—Hark ! they carol thro' the grove,

[Love unfettered, &c. D. Capo.

Jen. Ay, ma'm !—and I'd be as free as the lark
myfelf, if I had the fortune that you'll have, and not
be mew'd up any longer.

Nar. But there's fuch a thing as reputation, Jenny ;—and my father never fails to tell me, 'tis to be
preferved but by prudence and philofophy.

Jen. Philofophy ! what the deuce does he mean by
that ?

Nar. That I fhould fubdue all my feelings I fuppofe, in compliment to his.

Jen. Is that his philofophy ?—oh never think of it,
ma'm, 'till you can think of nothing elfe.———I dare
fwear your papa never thought any thing about it, 'till
he found himfelf a philofopher againft his will.

A I R V. *Mrs. Wrighten.*

Since his worfhip forfooth,
Having loft his fweet tooth,
Forbids you Love's feaft
Which no more he can tafte,
Be advis'd, and he'll find you a tartar !
Talk of lovers to vex him :
Intrigue to perplex him :—
What give nature the lye?
By my ftars would not I !
'Though I dy'd the next moment her martyr.

Nar.

Nar. There's fomething of reafon in that girl ;—
or rather, there's fomething in it I believe that flat-
ters my own inclinations :—be that as it may ;—me-
thinks if *Byron* were prefent, I fhould not hefitate to
fly with him any where.

Jen. Lud ma'm ! if you could but behold yourfelf
this moment, you'd fee the charming difference between a defpairing damfel, and one who loves with
fpirit :—for my part, I always think it time enough
for a woman to defpair, when you may count her age
by her wrinkles.

Nar. Thy pleafantry, girl, generally carries confo-
lation along with it :—Well ! tho' I cannot but fome-
times lament his abfence, yet I receive comfort from
thy council, which tells me, I fhall one day or other
fee a reverfe of fortune :—Oh ! how tranfporting the
idea, Jenny !

A I R   VI.   *Mrs. Baddely.*

Thus the midnight tempeft raging
    Strikes the failor with difmay,
Furious winds, and waves engaging,
    Banifh every hope of day !

But at dawn, their wrath fubfiding,
    Ocean wears a tranquil face ;
Joy, through every current gliding
    Calms his bofom into peace.

Jen. Hufh ! hufh !—As I hope to be married, yon-
der's that arch-mongrel *Spy* upon the watch behind the
mulberrry-tree there ; — and now he's coming this
                                        way.—

way :—what if I could prevail upon him to go down to the election, and make me deputy turnkey.

Nar. That's impossible; he gets too much by watching us, to give up his post for nothing.

Jen. Do you call love nothing ?—Consider what you feel yourself, madam, and then think of poor Spy's sufferings.—Ha! ha! ha!— he's dying for me; and so if he won't betray every body else to obey me, he shall dangle upon that willow before I give him a single grain of hope;—— however, take your book, and go rest yourself in your favourite bower near the fountain, while I try the power of my charms.—He must give up his master or me: so don't fear our success.

Nar. Prosper thee my faithful girl ! *[Exit* Nar.

Enter SPY.

Spy. Your servant, Madam Jenny : — its a blessed fine day, and you're all alone, I see.—I am with you indeed,—but then I'm nobody, Mrs. Jenny, unless you'd smile upon me.

Jen. Smile upon *you*, Mr. Spy ?—you are nobody indeed ;—can an English-woman, and a friend to liberty and the rights of the constitution, smile upon a creature——

Spy. Creature !—am I a creature, Mrs. Jenny ?—why you make me as bad as Dragon.

Jen. You are worse, Mr. Spy : he's a dumb creature, and knows no better ;—but you can talk, and talk finely, Mr. Spy.

Spy. Thank you for that, Mrs. Jenny :—to be sure I can talk a little when I am half cock'd.

Jen.

Jen. Fie for fhame! then, Mr. Spy!——Fie for fhame!—Can a freeborn woman like myfelf, who would give up my life, nay more—perhaps my honour for my country—

Spy. That is noble indeed!

Jenny. —Shall I fmile upon a creature, who, whilft his country's rights are in danger at the election of Tipplewell, can meanly, and ingloriously ftay at home to watch the motions of two innocent young ladies, when he fhou'd be huzzaing, drinking, and breaking windows, for liberty and property?—

Spy. Indeed, and fo I fhould:——how her fine fpeeches melt a body!

Jen. O fie for fhame, Mr. Spy!— never afk for my fmiles. My fmiles, my hand, and my heart fhall be given to a *man* only, and an *Englifhman*.

Spy. I am both a man and an Englifhman:—but what fignifies all that, when I've no money in my pocket:—if I had but one piece of filver to prime me with a little, no man fhould ftand firmer by you and his country, than little Spy would.

Jen. You fhant want for that then, tho' its the only companion to my filver thimble:—here Mr. Spy.

[*gives him money.*

Spy. Now one little roguifh fmile, that I'd give a thoufand of thefe for,—and the keys are your own.

Jen. Dearest Mr. Spy [*courtefying and fmiling*] I thank you!

Spy. Had they been the keys of the ftrong beer cellar, you fhould have had 'em!—thus I furrender up the garrifon for the prefent, [*giving her the keys*] and now to protect the laws, liberties, and property of Old England: [*going, returns.*]—Perhaps, Mrs. Jenny,

I may

I may return bold enough to intreat another favor,——
may I hope?

Jen. A patriot may hope——never to figh in vain!

Spy. That's noble again!——I'll only ftep and mount
my gaters, and return in an inftant;——you fhall let
me out at the back gate, and I'll whifk down to the
borough as quick as a nine-pounder

That——for my mafter!——by your fmiles I'm bleft,
Ale! love! and liberty, now fire my breaft.

[*Exit* Spy.

JENNY *laughing.*

Ha! ha! ha! there's a pretty fool now!—— If the
fate of a kingdom had depended upon it, the gudgeon
would have bit juft the fame.——Let fhort-fighted poli-
ticians fay what they will about the power of money,
a little well-diffembled love will go farther, take my
word for it.

[*Exit* Jenny.

SCENE

SCENE IV.

*A perspective view to the General's park; on an oak tree near the paling of which is the usual inscription of—*Men traps, and spring guns, &c.

Enter BYRON.

By this time the old buck is lost in the general uproar of an election .—What a lucky dog was I to catch a glimpse of him as he pass'd along the road !—let him choose whom he pleases,—I am happy that I refus'd the solicitations of my friends, as my success would but have increased his resentment.—Give me, kind Fortune, but thy voice in *Love's* soft election, and I care not who are the representatives of a tumultuous borough!—but here's the blest retreat of my Narcissa.

A I R VII. *Mr. Vernon.*

How oft through this responsive grove
    Has softest echo told my tale !
When e'er she caught my notes of love,
    She gently bore them down the vale }

The scene renew'd, my wakeful breast
    Now joyful beats to love's alarms ;
Ye powr's who pity the distrest,
    Transport me to *Narcissa's* arms !

————Heighday !—[*difcovering the infcription*]—what new bugbear have we here ?—" Men-traps and fpring-" guns fet in thefe grounds DAY and NIGHT."———— Well done general !—Indeed you plann'd things a little better laft war, or we fhould not have heard fo much of your exploits :—ha! ha! ha!—fuch a device might fecure your ducks and geefe, but not the game I'm in purfuit of, I affure you :—fo with my coufin Ranger—Up I go !—up I go!—[*getting upon the pales.*]—there—now if the Cyprian deity, has not taken care to draw all the charges of his fpring-guns, and blunt the teeth of his fteel-traps, I'm miftaken in my goddefs !—So love and fortune go with me.

[*jumps over.*

D   ACT.

ACT II.

SCENE V.

JENNY *alone.*

I Knew I could coax him to make a fool of himself, and give me the keys : — Hark! did not I
hear something ? No ; I believe it was only the noise
of the cascade : but it put my heart into my mouth !
—Egad, if Miss Narcissa was to be catch'd sleeping
—and the poor thing takes a very sound nap—there
would be a fine spot of work ; but I believe there's
no great danger, for the gardeners can't be come back
from the election yet :— Well, I'll e'en take a run
across the green, and see if I can spy him for her.—
Pretty creatures I should like to bring them together !
—and for all she's so sly, and looks so demure, my
word for it she'll have no objection.—If all women
were like me, they'd cut the matter very short, for my
tongue and my heart always go together.

AIR

AIR VIII. *Mrs. Wrighten.*

Fine ladies may tell us
They hate pretty fellows,
Defpife little Cupid—his quiver, and dart,
But when love's only by,
Not a prude will deny,
That man tho' a tyrant's the lord of her heart.
So bewitching a creature !
So noble each feature !
My bofom commands me to take his dear part ;
Then how can I conceal
What my eyes will reveal ?—
That he muft, and he will be—the lord of my heart.

SCENE

SCENE VI.

BYRON *difcovered in an attitude of furprife, beholding* NARCISSA *afleep in a Jeffamin bower.*

Byr. —Surely my eyes deceive me!—or is it fome fleeping Naiad of the neighbouring floods?—No; 'tis her! 'tis my Narciffa's beavenly form, harmonious form'd by nature's matchlefs hand!

AIR IX. *Mr. Vernon.*

My bofom's on fire!
It throbs with defire,
Say whither ye gods fhall I fly?
Love preffes my ftay;
But fhould I obey,
To my paffions a victim I die.

[going, returns.

———But ftay:—thus will I obey the dictates of honor as well as love. Thanks to loye and the defcriptive author of the *Seafons.* [*Takes a card from his pocket, and writes*] ———there:——in atonement for the innocent trefpafs on thy foft repofe, I will become thy watchful guardian, and protect thee from the eye of any rude obferver:—but foft! my eager tranfport has difturb'd her:—fhe wakes—and fee fhe fhrinks even at nature's voice;—alarm'd, and blufhing at the doubtful breeze! I muft conceal myfelf.

[He retires behind a tree.

NAR-

NARCISSA *awaking.*

Nar. ——Methought I heard fome human voice!
Thefe fleeplefs eyes, wearied with perpetual watchings,
betrayed me ito flumber :—Sure no eye profane peep'd
thro' yon clofe recefs, and in my unguarded moments————Ah! what's here? [*feeing the card*]——
then I'm undone. [*Comes forward and reads.*]

———— ———— "Sleep on my fair,
" Yet unbeheld, fave by the facred eye
" Of faithful love: I go to guard thy haunt,
" To keep from thy recefs each vagrant foot,
" And each licentious eye!"

[*After a paufe of wonder*]——It is – it is my Byron's
well-known hand!—then why thefe mixt emotions
hard to be defcrib'd? why heaves my labouring breaft,
except to bid eternal welcome to its long-lov'd lord?—
No, my Byron, no! thy virtuous merit fhall go no
longer unrewarded :—but where is he?—fled!—affift
me then love's favourite mufe, that thus expreffing my
own feelings, I may alleviate the feverity of his.—
[*She writes and fings.*]

AIR X. *Mrs. Baddely.*

Dear youth my fond heart you have won,
Tis a truth, that it cannot deny ;
Love's fetters have made us but one,
Then tell me,—ah! why didft thou fly?

My

My hand fhall thy honour repay,
As witnefs this amorous figh !
   So believe me when hither you ftray,
You need not,——

    [Byron difcovering himfelf fings—I never will fly !

Nar. [*dropping the card*] Heavens defend me !

Byr. Forgive me, lovely maid, for thus breaking in upon thofe angelic ftrains :— if I have miftaken their fweet harmonious burthen, I am fufficiently punifhed for my prefumption.

Nar. [*beholding him affectionately*] My faithful Byron ? —why fhould my tongue deny, what my looks, fighs, and every action of my life proclaim ?—In the infancy of affection, hypocrify may be merit; but when love is affured of love, concealment would be folly, and prudery a crime.

A I R   XI.

Mrs. Baddely and Mr. Vernon.

NAR. —Here I plight a maiden's vow !—
BYR. —By thy beauteous felf I fwear !—
NAR. Thou fhalt be my guardian now !
BYR. Thou fhalt be my only care !

DUET.

Here we plight, &c.—

Enter

Enter JENNY *haſtily.*

Jen. Oh, ſtop your piping!—who the deuce would have thought of ſeeing you here—[*to Byron*—Your papa, m'am, is this moment return'd, and Sir Harry Muff along with him ; they'll be in at the gate in the twinkling of an eye !

Nar. Oh we are undone then, what ſhall we do ?

Byr. How for your ſake ſhall I avoid them ?

Jen. Oh dear m'am, I have it !— run both of you with me into the temple, and I'll bolt you in ſafe enough :—I've been forced to play at bo-peep with him there a hundred and a hundred times before now myſelf——in | in | in !—

[*Exeunt to the temple.*

SCENE

SCENE VII.

Gen. WORRY, *and Sir* HARRY MUFF.

Sir Harry. No Sir ;—thefe things never give a moments uneafinefs to a man of the world, *Sur mon honeur.*

Gen. No ?—What the devil, be kick'd out of your birthright by an impudent young fcoundrel, the fecond fon of an obftinate fool of a baronet, and not take fire at it ? You'd make a damn'd fine foldier!———

Sir Harry. We take fire at nothing, *Gen.* Worry : You fine gentlemen of the laft century, wore yourfelves out with your gunpowder paffions before you were men :—for example, your fire has burnt you to the bone, General ; fo that you are in reality, nothing but a collection of tinder and touchwood.

Gen. Damme, you've not a fingle fpark of fire in your whole compofition.

Sir Harry. Paffion of any kind agitates the human frame moft horribly ; and therefore we of the high *ton* have no paffions at all ; indeed our lives may be properly ftiled, a kind of agreeable vegetation.

Gen. Agreeable vegetation !———what a devil of a hufband will this fellow make ?   [*afide.*

Sir Harry. But I'm all agog for a fight of your delicious daughter—they tell me fhe's a fine *cretur* ; is fhe any thing like Maria ?—[*Taking off his hat*]

Gen. What the devil has he got there ?—A picture in his hat inftead of a button !

Sir Harry. —Apropos, has *Narciffa* good teeth ?

Gen.

Gen. What the devil will he afk me next? [*afide*] I'll anfwer for't, fhe'll do your table no difcredit, if that's all ; — but zounds———

Sir Harry. Table| why my dear General, we do not underftand each other :—Do you ferioufly imagine, that teeth in this enlighten'd age, like your green handled knives and forks, are mechanically conftructed for eating ?

Gen. Why, what the devil would you have 'em conftructed for ?

Sir Harry. Quel fauvage! (*afide*) why General, if you muft know, the teeth belonging to perfons of fafhion, are tortur'd into beauteous femi-circles, and polifh'd thrice a day for the admiration of the beholders.

Gen. And that's the reafon, I fuppofe, why our fine Gentlemen are always upon the broad grin ;—a fet of flop dawdle puppies !

Sir Harry. Why, do you really think, General, that I fhould cut fo capital a figure in a fafhionable grin, if I had delv'd all my days in tough, old Englifh roaft beef ?

Gen. I tell you, I neither know nor care :—but one thing I fancy you'll find, that my daughter will not eafily be prevailed upon to give up her notions of fubftantials, in compliment to your delicate appetite.

Sir Harry. Oh leave that to me, General .—I fhall foon make a convert of her ; or why have I fcaled the lofty Alps, and fwept the aromatic vales of bleft Italia : —if Narciffa is fortunate enough to have a gufto for poetry and mufic, I fhall make a rapid conqueft.

Gen. Damn your mufic and poetry ! for both of you together, would turn Worry-Hall into a mad-houfe.

[*afide.*)

Sir

Sir Harry. You muſt know, General, that the Muſes all
Nine, ſmil'd upon my birth, and Apollo ſtood god-
father to me by proxy.

Gen. Damme, but I believe he's touch'd !   [*aſide.*

Sir Harry. I have written a ſong, that has made a
little noiſe in the polite world ;—and tach'd the crotchets to it myſelf.

Gen. His crotchets !——Oh he's paſt recovery.
[*aſide.*

Sir Harry. —Nay, the *Scavoire vivre*, of which I've
the honour to be a member, forc'd their annual prize
upon me for the compoſition.——You muſt know, we
were rallied a little upon a certain occaſion by the female wits of the *Coterie :* ſo you may gueſs who was
fix'd upon for our literary champion. *(affectedly)* You
ſhall have it, though it will loſe much of its effect, from
the preſſure of an Engliſh atmoſphere, upon the delicate organs of my pipe.

General (walking about haſtily,) mad as a March hare !

A I R   XII.   *Mr. Dodd.*

Ladies in vain,
    Why entertain,
Hopes to bewitch us with loves artful wiles ?
    Ceaſe to do ſo
    Since you all know,
We have his patent for dimples and ſmiles.

Gentler beaux that pow'r poſſeſſing
    Yield no more to your alarms,
Each his ſcented ſelf careſſing,
    Quite enamour'd with his charms !

Prettp

'Pretty playthings all adieu !
Now diffolve in am'rous fighs,
We a fofter clime purfue,
Froze too long beneath your eyes.

Da Cape.

Gen. —Pfhaw ! damn your finging, it may be very
fine, but I'm not in a humour to relifh it :—I'm
touch'd to the quick at being flung by the *Byrons* ;—
and yet you feem to mind it no more, than the lofs of a
match of billiards.

Sir Harry. My dear General, he compos'd as I am ;
—and don't fret yourfelf in this abfurd manner :——

Gen. I won't be compos'd ;—damme, but I will fret
myfelf !—Indeed if I was of your cucumber like difpo-
fition, you might expect to find me as fine a piece of
ftill life, agreeable vegitation as yourfelf ; but—no, no,
no, Sir !—

Sir Harry. Now indeed, General, I mean to refent
their treatment ; and to fhew you I'm in earneft, I'll
lodge a petition againft them by this light.

Gen. Ay ; why there you are right, for your grounds
are good enough :—

Sir Harry. 'Pon honour, General, you fhall be com-
manding officer for the day.

Gen. If that's the cafe, I have a plan :—but I'm
fo tir'd :—walk with me into the temple, and I'll tell
it to you :—I am fure we fhall difcover fome underhand dealings of this young rafcal's at the bottom, and
don't doubt of bringing it home to him. (*finding the
doors faft*)—What the devil's the meaning of this ?—
why the door's faften'd wi hin.—[*liftens at the key-hole*]
—Zounds ! here are fome villains concealed with a

E 2   defign

defign to rob the houfe; liften, Sir Harry, *(Sir Harry puts his ear to the door)* here Robbin! Matthew! Jerry!—why, where the devil are thefe fcoundrels got to?

Sir Harry. Why really, General, I do hear a kind of confederate buz;—   [*Enter Robbin.*

Rob. What's your honour's will?

Gen. Here, break open the door directly:—fome thieves have hid themfelves within fide!——

Rob. Have they, your worfhip?—then we'll foon have them out.—Come along my boys! *(Enter* Mat. *and* Jerry.)—Thieves in our garden! we'll let 'em know that nobody fhall encroach upon our privileges, without a good ducking, however;——

[*They burft open the door with their fpades, and difcover Byron:—the gardeners laugh.*]

Gen. —Hell and the devil! what have we got here? —your feryant, Mr. Byron:—I give you joy of your election, Sir!—*(fneeringly)*—how compos'd the raf-cal ftands!—what, I fuppofe, you are a ftick of agree-able vegitation too?

Sir Harry. This is rather too much, damme! upon his return for one borough, to be canvaffing for ano-ther:—Don't you fmoak a pettycoat, General?

[*The General looking inquifitively.*]

Byr. Gentlemen, my prefent fituation prevents me from returning your raillery:—

Gen. Fire! and fmoke! my daughter's maid Jenny! —why huffy, how dare you be lock'd up with fuch a rake as this.

Jen. Law Sir! the gentleman only afk'd to fee the temple, and fo I thought there was no harm in fhewing it him.

Sir Harry. Comingly kind, by all that's plump, and lovely !

Gen. How the devil did he get in when the gates were all lock'd ?—but it's a lye, huffy, he came caterwauling after you ; but get about your bufinefs, you jade ! you fhan't ftay in my houfe another minute !—

Byr. Nay then, Sir, I hope it will not offend you, fince it can no longer be concealed, if I produce the moft delicate teftimony of our innocence.—

[*Stepping back difcovers* Narciffa.]

Sir Harry. Doublets by this light !

Gen. Narciffa ! Traytor ! deliver up my daughter, whom you have feduced, that I may punifh her as fhe deferves !

Byr. Retire Narciffa, into the citadel, I befeech you, and I'll defend you to the laft :—

Narc. I beg you'll give me up, your danger overpowers me. [*To Byron.*]

Jen. Dear Ma'm, you are only to reward the conqueror ; you have nothing to do with the battle :—befides, Mr. *Muff* will take care there fhan't be much blood fpilt.—

Gen. Matchlefs impudence !—what ! laugh'd at into the bargain ?—Seize him, *Robin*, and drag him to the canal :—Rafcals, why don't you obey my orders ?

Rob. What ! duck young Mafter *Byron* :—not I, I love him too well ?—

Other gardeners. And fo do I :—

Gen. Villains, you are my flaves ; and I'll make you do what I command you :—lay hold on him, I fay !

AIR

A I R XIII.

TRIO. *Mr. Bannifter, Mr. Faweet, and Mr. Kear.*

He's the pride of the borough, god blefs him fay I!
I've poll'd for his honour, and will till I die.;
  In vain then you rave,
  I'll not be your flave,
Tho' I'm a poor fellow of humble degeee:
  Which of you then will bear it?
  Will you?
 — MAT. No I fwear it!
Or you? JERRY. No I fwear it!
There is but one way then to fet us all free:
 We'll none of us bear it:
 Will you?—*both*—No, I fwear it:
Nor BOB, I declare it:
This, this is the way then, for now we are free.

       [*Throw down their fpades, &c.*]

 Eyr. You muft excufe me Gen'ral, though I am un.
er the neceffity even in this place, of defending your
daughter, from any violence on her inclinations.

 Gen. Scoundrels! I'll be revenged! Oh! here comes
Spy!—fetch my double-barrel'd horfe-piftols this inftant; why the rafcal's drunk! [*Enter Spy.*]

 Spy. *Byron* for ever! fhoot who, him?—Lord love
his heart—*Byron* for ever!—I tell you that won't do:—
there's no flints:—I would not hurt a hair of his head.
—*Byron* for ever!—(*turning to Sir Harry*)—So I think
we wa'n't troubled to chair your fine gingerbread car-
cafe:—damme, you know'd a trick worth too of that!

              Sir

Sir Harry. Filthy brute !

Gen. The devil has bewitched 'em, all to confpire againft me ! Get out of my fight, villain, or I fhall be the death of you :—

Spy. Oh ! if that's all—I can punch it :—*Byron* for ever !—tho' he don't want a fecond :—he's fpunk : —he can manage 'em both—No Muffs and Indigo Nabobs—*Byron* for ever !—   [*Exit reeling.*]

Gen. Powder and fury ! I believe there's neither a brave, nor an honeft man left in the kingdom.—Look you, Sir *Harry*, win her and wear her :—What ! I fuppofe, I muft fight this fellow myfelf *(goes up to the door)* but here he comes,—if he refufes to furrender her, put him to death !

Sir Harry. Well, if it muft be fo, it muft ; tho' 'pon my foul, I've no butchering ideas about me *(half draws)* —come, good Sir, don't put me to the fatigue of chaf- tifing you.

Byr. Sir *Harry*, you have more humanity : —

Sir Harry. No, fplit me if I have !—She's mine by deed of gift ; if you difpute that title, fhe muft be mine by force of arms ;—*(Draws, and puts himfelf in an attitude.)*

Byr. Say you fo ?—come on then :—*(drawing a piftol, Sir* Harry *fprings back.)*

Gen. Why, what the devil, are you afraid of the fmell of powder ?   [*To Sir Harry.*

Sir Harry. No, not in the leaft, General, (confufedly) —I am—I am—only difconcerted a little for,—for fear of the ladies ;—you faw they retired diforder'd : befides, Sir, I'm not upon an equal footing with the affaffin.

Byr. No more you were, when you valiantly drew
upon

upon a naked man. :—however, Sir, not to alarm you with the superiority of my weapon, thus I resign it into your hands [*Sir Harry receives the pistol, cocks it, and advances.*

Sir Harry. Oh then the citadel's our own General !

Byr. When you have won it, Sir ! *(presents a second pistol.*

Sir Harry. [*Retiring affrighted.*] Split me, but the ruffian has got another !

Gen. [*looking earnestly at Byron*] Damme, that's noble too ! It's almost a sin to kill so fine a fellow :— but the calls of honor must be obey'd :—come, you shall settle it like soldiers however :—I little thought I should ever see another shot fired, *(measures ten paces with his cane,*

Sir. Harry. My dear General, what are you about ?

Gen. About ? — Why measuring the ground :— you would not fight like a couple of foot-pads, with the muzzle of the pistol in each others mouth, would you ? What the devil ails you now ?

Sir. Harry. Dear General, your ear a moment *(whispering,* my conscience forbids me.

Gen. Conscience ! who the devil ever heard of a man's having conscience, who had no heart ?—however, Sir *Harry,* I see how the land lies :—You need give yourself no further concern about me or my family :—I am determin'd to have a brave man for my son-in-law, tho' I cross the ocean for him.

Byr. You need not put yourself to that inconveniency, Sir, when you behold in me, one, who is ready to lay down his life in defence of your daughter's virtue, and your honor.

Gen. Why, tho' my enemy—thou art a fine fellow I own :—and if I could forget the family grudge——

Byr.

Byr. Believe me, Sir, I have lamented in secret the groundlefs animofity, that has fo long fubfifted between you and my father, fo fatal to the early overtures I made the lovely *Narciffa*.

Gen. Zounds! but when I recollect, — to be jockey'd by you out of the borough. and by fuch underhand means !—

Byr. Why; Sir, you furprize me !—they have chofen that Gentleman, have they not ? [*pointing to Sir Harry*.]

Gen. No, Sir, they have not. — what, you don't know, I fuppofe, that they have return'd you ?

Byr. Upon my honour, no, Sir: —I have been employ'd upon a much more agreeable fervice :—and to convince you of it, as they have chofen me, contrary to my wifhes, I am ready to refign my feat in favour of any one, you fhall appoint.

Gen. No, you young dog: — you fhan't do that neither : —I am a little cooler than I was :—that piece of ftill life there, has brought me to my fenfes: [*pointing to Sir Harry*] I begin now to think, that the unanimous choice of a free body of people, is too facred, to be fuperceded by the will of any individual; befides your courage has charm'd me:— come, you young dog, you may releafe your prifoners, they fhall be upon their parole, 'till I pafs fentence. [*Byron opens the door of the temple, and brings them a little forward*.] You look mighty cunning, Sir *Harry*, after loofing *Tipplewell*, and the richeft heirefs in the county , through your delicate feelings.— damn fuch feelings, fay I ! you'll cut a pretty figure in the modern hiftory of Maccaronyifm !

Sir Har. Why, good General, you don't know me yet :—I confefs I have loft a pair of pretty toys !—— but with refpect to your modern fatire, a real fine gen-

F   tleman,

tleman, is infinitely beyond it's reach, I affure you :—,
fo I fhall laugh at the dinner-hunting tribe.·

Gen. Why, where the devil did this fellow fpring
from !—*(Byron, Jenny,* and *Narciffa, coming forward)*—I ·
believe the young rogue deals in magic with both of us—
(to *Narciffa)*—come hither, girl, don't tremble fo :—I .
begin to think, that I've held out too long with Sir
Walter—and therefore I don't know how I can fhew
a heartier defire of reconciliation, than by rewarding
his fon of merit, with my only daughter and fifty ·
thoufand pounds :—What fays Narciffa ?—but I need
not afk her !—

Nar. If I may difcover my partiality for Mr. Byron,
without offending you, Sir, I fhould tell you, that I
have every reafon in the world to admire and efteem him.

Gen. Come hither, then, both of you ; as an earneft
of my approbation, there—I've joined your hands before the parfon ; and may neither you, nor I live to
repent it.

Byr. This, Sir, is fo generous, my life will be too
fhort to repay the obligation.

Sir Har. Demme, but I cut a pretty figure here truly !
——chous'd out of my own borough, and a fine girl,
by the fon of a fox-hunting baronet ;—and laughed at
by the old Jew of a father, for endeavouring to accom-
modate him !—Well !—What's to be done ?—Why,
upon my arrival at Almack's, I muft carry it off, for
the prefent, by dint of bronze ; tell 'em the girl was
damn'd ugly ; and, that the other borough had loft it's
charter.

Gen. Come, come, Sir Harry ; every man's not born ·
to be a giant-killer ;—(*ironically*) if it be not beneath
the dignity of a fine gentleman, to rejoice at the fuccefs

of ·

of a worthier man than himself, adjourn with us to
Worry-hall.

Sir Har. Any thing for a frolic, General, for I'm in
tip-top spirits.

Gen. All that now remains, is for me to endeavour
to prevail upon Sir Walter to meet us, and confent to
make the little rogues happy :—for my own part, I am
now fully convinced, that the tender affections were
never implanted in the human breaft, to be call'd forth,
or fuppreffed, by the caprice of an unfeeling parent.

VAUDEVILLE.

NARCISSA.

Rofy archer come away !
Give your train a holiday,
Lay your bow and quiver by,
Ceafe to wound,—and hither hie !

CHORUS.

Rofy archer, &c.

BYRON.

Hither bring the fmiling graces,
And the loves with cherub faces,
Bid the valleys laugh and fay,
" Love has made a holiday!"

CHORUS.
Hither bring, &c.

SIR

SIR HARRY.

Lips of coral! eyes so pretty !
    Out of luck foregad was I :
Tho' I'm chous'd, I'll join the ditty
    Down thou little rising sigh.
May Love's tender prittle-prattle
    Keep the day for ever bright,
And no jealous tittle-tattle,
    Mar the raptures of the night !

CHORUS.

May Love's tender, &c.

JENNY.

Gentlefolks if you'll permit me
    I've a word or two to say,
Tho' perhaps it mayn't befit me,
    On my lady's wedding-day :
Gravest Don with eye of ferrit
    Tho' he practise all his art,
Cannot break a woman's spirit,
    Till he's strength to break her heart.

CHORUS.

Gravest Don, &c.

COLONEL WORRY.

Brother grey-beards short's my story,
    Read your features in this glass,
Here's a convert now before ye
    Metamorphos'd from an ass :——
                                When

When a fwain of merit woos her,
   Make your girl a happy wife ;
Nature bids you not refufe her,
   In the CRISIS of her life.

CHORUS.

When a fwain of merit woos her,
   Make your girl a happy wife ;
Nature bids you not refufe her,
   In the CRISIS of her life !

THE END.

EPILOGUE.

EPILOGUE.

Written by the AUTHOR,

AND SPOKEN BY

Mr. WESTON,

Entering with a large Dog.

OH! Lud! What authors have we now adays!
    A farmer this! —Ecod or what you pleafe:
He fwears (tho' we've but juft got thro' one fweat-o)
He'll make us fpeak an epilogue duetto.—
What fay you *Dragon?*—Why's your tail fo low?—
Be not chop-fall'n—they can't damn *you*, you know:—
What dumb my comrade?—terrible difafter;
So I muft puff for you, and for your mafter.
Ye Gods be kind!—No cat-call interference!
Believe, *Tom Wefton*, 'tis his firft appearance.—

    You would not think it; but the rogue's fo fteady,
He's in the privy-council here, already;
The *Prompter* gives him merit univerfal,
Becaufe—[*whiftling*] his whiftle calls him to rehearfal;
Befides, he imitates no tragic brother,—
Who makes him pull down one bill—poft another;
Tho' he's not fleek;—and has an hungry eye,
(A poet's dog is never fed too high)
Yet he is found, Sirs, and in good condition;
He has no whimfies—no indifpofition:
When e'er in letters large the bills he graces,
You're fure of feeing him—if you have places;
He'll *top* the bills, if to this text he fticks;
A dog of parts—and have no puppy tricks?—
                     Odzooks,

EPILOGUE.

Odzooks, I've loſt his buſineſs in his praiſe;
Oh!—here he's ſent to guard his maſter's bays.
A *Dragon*, once they ſay, kept watch and ward,
Some curious golden fruit from thieves to guard.
So to protect the poet's fruit from riot,
Secure ſome guineas, and a better diet,
He's ſent this *Dragon* critics!—So be quiet:
Sharp then's the word, my ſlender waiſted couſins,
He'll ſwallow macaronies by the dozens!
Growling, and ſnarling,—don't let this dog catch ye,
At all your tearing-work he'll over match ye;
If by ill humours, you our bard wou'd puzzle,
I've nothing elſe to do—but ſlip the muzzle!
Tho' your ſo high *(to the galleries) You too* he ſoon
        wou'd tame;
DRAGON has wings, if I but ſhew him game.
    But ſhou'd his maſter's ſing-ſong melt your ſoul,
He'll be as ſoft as—*Signor Roſignol:*
Will with harmonious howlings ſwell each note,
And bark ſweet muſic—" *only from his throat.*"

www.ingramcontent.com/pod-product-compliance
Lightning Source LLC
Chambersburg PA
CBHW021246260626
47172CB00002B/854